Empire's Fall
The Prequil To Empire's Ghost

TLS

ISBN: 978-1-959350-52-1
Set in: Georgia 10pt, Brigstone 20pt, Victoriandeco Italic 30pt

©The Three Little Sisters LLC
USA/Canada

Author's note: the events in this story happen approximately twelve years before those described in Empire's Ghost.

Once to Every Man and Nation

The boy slept quietly against Thorazan's shoulder as he glided through the whispering woods, his footfalls silent under the murmuring of the wind in the trees, the gentle plashing of the brooks, the rustling of deer and foxes through the underbrush. Although the thick leaves above blotted out most of the light of Moon and stars, he walked as easily as a captain on his own deck, his sense of the land eddying around rocks and fallen logs, wafting him over the tangles and vines that would have clutched at another man's ankles. And always, always, pricking up as carefully as the ears of stag and wolf for the hint of other human presences, outlaws or enemies or even the allies to whom he must not surrender the boy.

Three more days, and we will be safe, Thorazan told himself. Tharandrost's northernmost garrison in Norwathe was not so far now, not after two weeks of shepherding the boy back through the woods without others taking his prize from him - for love, for the outlaws' foul purposes, for political effect: it did not matter. Tharandrost wanted the boy; and Thorazan was loyal to his country. The boy shifted in his sleep, his head rolling trustingly against Thorazan's shoulder.

His weight - no more than eighty or ninety pounds, for all his lanky height - was nothing to the Tharandrostan; but his long limbs were awkward to manage. The boy...

The whelp, Thorazan reminded himself. He is a Plainsman; he is my captive. But it was hard to remember when he could feel the boy's sleeping mind flowing easily through the damp earth and coursing sap, as much a part of the woods as the owl drifting silent-winged overhead...or Thorazan himself, guided silently through the forest not by eyes or ears or scent, but by the land-sense that melded and reached past all of them, the awareness of the earth itself rushing around and through him like a great river. The mission had seemed simple at first...

"Your duty," Commander Darzarak said, "is to scout around the north, this way." The Commander's slim finger traced a high arc on the map, past the golden counters marking Kantar's troops and the blue ones showing the units Tharandrost had sent to its ally's aid, skirting around the known Plainsman settlements and the red wooden rondels indicating the rebel clans' hosts. "We have reason to think that some of their Oak-Men have retreated deep into the woods. With ordinary war-magic, there would be nothing to fear from them; but the distance at which the Oak-Men can rouse their earth-spirits is unknown. They may also have taken members of the chieftains' immediate families with them, and if that is the case, we must know. Else extirpation now will not suffice: the threat of rebellion will remain for generations, so long as the bloodlines they reverence survive." Darzarak sniffed, tossing his head to settle his shining black hair about his shoulders.

The commander's features showed all Tharandrost's pride in its own breeding, kept pure since the Empire's Fall and carefully controlled to strengthen the gifts of the Imperial race. Darzarak's contempt for the Plainsmen sharpened the taut lines of his pale fine-boned face; his slanted eyes narrowed until the thin lines of amber brightness ringing his pupils were barely sparks against the steel-gray irises.

"We have already proven that your peculiar talent keeps the Oak-Men from recognising you as a foreign presence, while you can detect them. So long as you keep physically out of sight, you should be able to find out much of what we need to know. Do you understand?"

"Yes, sir," Thorazan answered.

"Do not attempt to capture any of the Oak-Men. You are not qualified to control a prisoner of such powers. Kill them if you can do so without betraying your presence. However, if they have taken chieftains' family members to safety, such persons would be of value, and within your capacity to control. If you acquire a captive, get it back to us - only to us. Not Kantar! If it comes down to surrendering a prisoner to Kantarean forces - or anyone else - you are ordered to kill it first."

"Yes, sir," Thorazan repeated. The prospect of killing a Plainsman prisoner did not bother him unduly; rather less, indeed, than the idea that he might have to drag a wild Plainsman back over close to an hundred and fifty miles of rough territory by himself. If he had been gifted with Mind-Control, it would have been no problem; but his own talent, useful as it was for the scout's duties to which it had destined him, was a subtler one.

Well, Thorazan thought, I've managed to keep him safe so far. The boy murmured something sleepy in his own tongue, nuzzling his face into Thorazan's mottled cloak against the cool dampness of the night air. The Tharandrostan paused a moment, making sure his captive was wrapped comfortably, then walked on. Although I would rather have killed him at first.

A week into Thorazan's journey, Commander Darzarak spoke in his mind, directing him to join the Kantarean relief forces marching to Flintwall Keep - a small fortified mansion with a village below it, which had been serving as an occasional base and resupply point for Kantarean forces. The Plainsmen had chosen their time carefully, waiting until the soldiers had marched to join another attack fifty miles away.

Then...the stone walls had broken beneath the Oak-Men's magic, lying crumbled and overgrown by vines as though they had fallen three hundred years past. But the headless bodies, those that had not been gnawed apart or carried off by dogs and swine and wolves, were fresh enough for Thorazan to see what the Plainsmen had done to their victims. The mutilations the males had suffered were bad enough; Thorazan felt his testicles trying to shrink back into the safety of his body.

Still, it was war, and one could expect no better from savages. But among the men, women's corpses also lay sprawled and naked, crusted pools of dried blood between their thighs and... pieces cut from them. They were only of the Common race, Thorazan reminded himself, maybe of Plainsman descent themselves. Not Imperials, not even the diluted blood of Kantar. It did not help. His mind might discount the victims' worth; but when he saw the proof that one young woman, at least, had been pregnant, his reaction boiled up from his guts, and he was barely able to turn aside before adding further insult to the pitiful body in front of him.

The Kantarean sergeant who had reluctantly accepted Thorazan's presence there laughed, though even in his shock, Thorazan could hear the hollow bitterness in the sound. "No stomach for battle-leavings, Tharandrostan?" the sergeant asked.

Like most Kantareans, the sergeant was very tall, five foot nine or so. Thorazan looked up coldly at him, noticing how dark the faint spattering of freckles spread over his cheeks on either side of his helm's nasal seemed. Mocking me to strengthen his own heart, Thorazan thought. The Tharandrostan was probably fifty years older than the other man - if a little younger in proportion to his lifespan - likely better-born, and certainly far better-educated.

Still, he could think of no clever reply, only, "They should not have killed the women. Or done...They are mad beasts; they deserve to die."

"Heh. True enough," the sergeant replied. He looked around. "Quicker to burn so many than to bury them. You're a bit small for carrying boulders or bodies; why don't you start cutting firewood?"

Thorazan might have shown him differently: the Kantarean sergeant might have three inches and a good two stone on him, but Thorazan could easily have lifted any of the fallen chunks of mortared flint-nuggets that took two or three Kantareans to move. However, he did not want to touch the corpses. He was shaking so badly, and felt so sick, that he had to walk out of sight to sit down for a few moments.

At least - whatever horrors the Plainsmen had committed on the bodies of their victims -their Oak-Men had done something to make sure no unquiet spirits lingered in Shadow. Twice Thorazan, wandering in the woods, had brushed against the outer edge of an Undead's circle of Shadow-fear. The breach in the walls of the green earth had disturbed his land-sense almost enough to make him ill. But here - appalling as the slaughter, rape, torture might be -he earth lay quiet, no more disturbed by the human blood that had soaked into it than it might be by the blood of a rabbit spattering from the blow of a hawk's talons. Thorazan thanked the gods: he felt he could not have borne the land's sickness at the taint of Shadow as well as his own.

Report, Darzarak said into Thorazan's mind. The scout took a deep breath to calm himself, and began his account. Remember, the Commander ordered after Thorazan had walked into the ruins of the manse itself and seen what the Plainsmen had done to its Imperial-blooded rulers, a captive - if it is the right captive - will be more valuable to us than a corpse. Even Darzarak's cool mindvoice sounded shaken: among a race that bred so slowly and with such difficulty, there was no crime greater than killing a fertile woman or child, with rape being a close second. Leave the Kantareans to their work now.

Thank you, sir, Thorazan replied. He rose from the rough-edged piece of mortared flint he was sitting on and began to walk north again, hoping that he would find a Plainsman to kill. Thorazan's arms were beginning to ache from the discomfort of holding the boy, and his steps were slowing. He shifted the child's position; the boy murmured something again, but did not wake. And then I nearly killed him accidentally, poor thing. As Thorazan neared the top of his arc, his progress slowed. It was true that the Oak-Men's land-sense would not reveal him as a stranger: his gift was common enough among Plainsmen and Common Men, but for Imperials - no. In Tharandrost, land-sense was a wild talent, a sport; the House of Procreation could not even work out its configuration well enough to propagate it.

Whereas much of the Plainsman magic was actually based on landsense expanded to a primitive shamanism, communing with those spirits or elementals that - if Thorazan sensed them at all - were no more than the faintest whispers at the edge of his awareness.

Still, though the Oak-Men might take Thorazan as one of their own by sense, sight would give him away at once. The mottled green of the scout's cloak made it easy for him to vanish in the forest, but if anyone got a clear glance - the hood might hide his black hair, shadowing his slanted eyes and delicately chiseled features. But the Plainsmen were a very tall people, often overtopping six feet; Thorazan was barely five foot six, and too broad-shouldered to pass as a boy even from a distance. Nor could he answer a hail, for though he spoke their languages well, his accent was unmistakable. So he hid and crept, circling carefully wide whenever the awareness of another human brushed against the furthest edges of his own sense.

Dusk was just falling, the deer stepping carefully from their beds to graze on the tender summer shoots as crows and robins settled into their nests, when Thorazan felt the unmistakable tingle of power growing to his left, drawing his awareness like a lodestone. It felt like a spring rising from the depths of the earth to spread into a pool of rich loamy water, like sap tingling swiftly through his veins as though spring were bursting from winter in moments instead of months...He might have stood in the humming thrall of the power, listening rapt until the work was done. But half a mile away, a family of wolves were padding hungry from their den.

Their desire for the hunt - deer-scent on the wind, blood-strong meat in their mouths, reminded Thorazan of his own predatory goal. Mind cleared, Thorazan knew what he was feeling: the Oak-Men were doing something, and whatever it was, he should stop it. And few things were more vulnerable than a mage caught up in his magics. The scout slipped along the overgrown trail, flowing silently between the thorny tangles of bushes, peeping around the thick trunk of a tall beech at the two men who stood before the tall stone.

Thorazan could feel the stone like an anchor, carved swirls and spirals echoing the subtle whirlings of the land's power all around, catching it and magnifying it and rooting it firmly in the earth again. The Oak-Men had their backs to him: a tangle of ruddy-gray hair flowed down over one man's white robe, badger-brindled over the other. Their power tugged at his own, calling him to open past the first fireflies' glimmer in the purple dusk, past the coolness of the damp earth under his feet and the smooth gray beech-bark against his cheek, to something that tingled just beyond his awareness, to faint voices singing a song that drew at his heart with longing...

Thorazan loosed, nocked, and drew again. The first Oak-Man was crumpling; the second just turning, his startling green eyes and dark-bearded mouth open with surprise, when the Tharandrostan's arrow took him in the throat. The power drained back into the earth with the dead men's blood, a quiet thrumming at the ends of Thorazan's nerves. Only then, as the tide of land-strength eased, did Thorazan sense the third presence, fainter and further off.

The scout did not stop to examine the bodies: he had been strictly warned against touching any items of Plainsman magic, on the chance that his talent would make him more vulnerable than most. Instead, he crept away, following the thin trace. It grew stronger as Thorazan came closer, drawing a veil of power about itself like a cloak.

The Plainsman has realized something happened to its comrades, he thought. And is trying to hide by becoming part of the woods. Thorazan had done the same, often enough; anyone who lacked his gift could stare right at him and never see him when he wrapped himself in the earth-sense. But he could tell...

Often enough, wolves missed their kill or hawks misjudged their stoops. Senses seeking for a power as great as that of the two Oak-Men he had slain, Thorazan realized that he was looking straight at the gray cloak and ruddy hair of the third Plainsman.

The Plainsman buck's green eyes opened wide, meeting his gaze. Suddenly it whirled and ran, Thorazan's arrow thunking into a tree behind it. Dropping the bow, Thorazan was on his quarry at once. It turned unexpectedly, and the Tharandrostan had no time to draw his sword; the two of them crashed down in an undignified heap, scrabbling in the grass. Thorazan saw the flash of a knife, and grabbed the Plainsman's wrist, squeezing until his enemy let out a sharp cry and dropped the weapon.

The frantic haste of combat fading from his brain, Thorazan realized that the Plainsman was struggling helplessly under his own weight; and that, weak as the Plainsman race was at its best, his captive's efforts to get free felt more like a sparrow's than a man's. He looked down into the buck's face...beardless as his own; and wild Plainsmen cultivated the hair that disfigured their features as early as they could.

Dear Aviyani, it's only a child! Thorazan thought. A child of...he tried to guess, remembering the difference in lifespans. No closer to manhood than his own son; a Tharandrostan in his mid-thirties would be the equivalent of...eleven or twelve for a Plainsman, perhaps? Certainly not old enough to be a magical threat; quite possibly the sort of captive he was ordered to take.

Thorazan shifted his grip and grabbed the whelp's other wrist. Scrawny as it was, it already had the large bones of its race, and the Tharandrostan's hand was not quite big enough to hold both wrists together. What do I do now? I can't tie it up while I'm holding it with both hands?

The sensible thing would be to knock the whelp out, but Thorazan hesitated, remembering his briefings. Plainsman bones were large, but fragile: a blow to the temple might crush his captive's skull. And...What idiot in the past, he wondered, decided that unarmed fighting was only fit for women? There were one-handed holds to control a prisoner for easy restraint, places where a controlled strike would subdue without much harm - and he had no idea how they worked; he only knew the breaking and grappling moves complementing close-in swordplay.

But if I don't do something, we'll lie here until his friends find us, or we both starve. Thorazan let go of one wrist and slapped the whelp gingerly on the edge of the jaw. The only response was another frenzy of weak struggles as the Plainsman clawed about for its knife with his free hand. Thorazan bit his lip and struck his captive harder. The whelp went limp, moaning softly.

Aviyani, have I broken it? he thought. At least the whelp was still alive. Thorazan tied it carefully and picked up the scrawny body, amazed at how light it was. The whelp was nearly as tall as he was, and he would be amazed if it were three-quarters of his own weight.

Worms, the Tharandrostan thought. I'll wager it needs worming...not to mention the fleas, the lice, and gods know what else. It didn't seem to smell too bad - though that was likely because, so long in the wilds, he was filthy as a Plainsman himself.

Thorazan walked for almost three candlemarks, then lit a small fire. His captive was awake, but seemed in too much pain to struggle any more, the side of its face badly swollen and purpled.

"Can you speak?" he asked.

The grunts of pain convinced Thorazan that he had broken the whelp's jaw. He thought unhappily of the healing potions in his pack. There was only one dose of boneheal, and if he broke a bone on the way back and didn't have it...

But I can't make a child walk with a broken jaw. I should have been more careful. If I'd thought to hold a weapon to its throat, to use threats instead of force...

He went to his pack and dug out the little case with the phials in their padded loops.

Boneheal, and...Poppy syrup. He'll still be in pain until it's fully set.

"This will make you better," Thorazan promised the young Plainsman. Green eyes met his

own in a glare of hatred. "It's not poison. If I wanted to kill you, you'd be dead."

The glare muted to a look of dubious consideration, then a whimpering nod. Thorazan uncorked the poppy syrup first. "This will ease the pain. The next one will heal your face. I don't have any more, so if you spit them out, that's it. Understand?"

To his relief, however, the whelp took the medicines without any effort to resist. Thorazan knew enough field medicine to tie the broken jaw up so that it could set properly; he built the fire as high as he dared, and wrapped his captive up in his own thin bedroll to keep him warm while he healed.

By the next morning, Thorazan was able to take the bandage off. He untied the whelp's legs as well, though he left his hands tethered.

"Who are you?" his prisoner asked. "Where are you taking me?"

"Suppose you answer my questions first? I did capture you, after all."

The Plainsman thought about that. "I guess that's fair.Ymwra's Blood, you have a strong

arm! Even my da can't hit that hard."

"I trust he wouldn't hit you that hard!" Thorazan said in shock.

His captive laughed. "He hits me plenty hard. But I never cry. I didn't cry when you hit me last night, either."

They are beasts, Thorazan thought. "Who is your father?" he asked carefully.

"My father is Avain the Gwyrothi of Clan Gwyrothi," the boy declared. "I am Rhodri of

Gwyrothi, the oldest and strongest of his sons, and everyone says I'm the likeliest to take the chieftainship after him. No one has ever bested my father in single combat, nor in songmaking nor in the drinking of mead nor the eating of meat, and even the Oak-Men call him cunning. And I shall grow up to be just like him."

Thorazan looked at Rhodri's scrawny body - he could almost count the ribs through the dirty gray wool of the boy's tunic - and thought, You haven't done too much eating lately. And if you're the strongest of your father's sons, I'd hate to see what the rest of them look like. Though he was willing, albeit unhappily, to believe that the Gwyrothi might beat his children.

"I hope not," the Tharandrostan murmured in his own tongue. Aloud, he asked, "What are you doing so far from home?"

"I'd planned to sneak out and drive Madoc's chariot in battle. He said he'd let me, but one of my uncles overheard, and they made me come up here with the Oak-Men. So I'd be safe."

Rhodri spat into the underbrush. "But..." He looked at Thorazan, and suddenly his broadboned face went pale beneath dirt and freckles, round green eyes very wide. "I felt them go last night. Their strength sank into the earth and then...did you kill them?"

"Yes," Thorazan said.

The boy drew away, as far as the rope would let him, staring in horror. "The hand that slays an Oak-Man is cursed," Rhodri said. "The land-spirits will turn against you, the..."

"Does it feel to you as though the land has turned against me?" Thorazan enquired gently.

The feeling of the boy's awareness trembling out through the earth, through his own landsense, was oddly soothing, almost familiar...When Thorazan's son Thoramar had been a few years younger, the boy would lay his head in his father's lap to sleep, and Indamith would nestle in close to her husband and son, the faint lavender-washed scent of her long black hair rising like an embrace around both of them.

"No," Rhodri whispered. "But how...?"

"Aviyani loves all her children," Thorazan said. "She does not curse the bear that kills an elk, nor the wolf-pack that drives out a stranger. Your Oak-Men raised no warding for me to violate, and I used no magic to kill them. Nor did I defile their holy stead or bodies. An angry bear or boar might have done as much."

"Our clan will have to avenge them," Rhodri said, straightening his back.

"They may try."

The boy looked around uneasily, wary as a fawn parted from the doe. "How can you touch the land?" he asked. "I had heard that your kind hates the earth, binding it with stone and chopping down all the woods for your ships."

"It was long ago when we ceased to destroy the forests for ships and began to tend them instead." At least fifteen hundred years; but it was true that the Empire had deforested a good part of the Middle Land for its mighty fleets. "And the Imperial race does not hate the earth, but...Our forebears, the Wheel-Folk, lived as the Horse-Tribes do, as mounted wanderers.

Then they were given rule over those who dwelt in the West; hence they never needed landsense.

Only a few of us have it." In Tharandrost, only myself. The few Imperial Kantareans with the gift likely got it from Plainsman or Common ancestors. Even Thoramar...even my own son lacks it, despite all the House of Procreation could do.

"What's wrong?" Rhodri asked.

"Nothing."

"I can feel it," the boy insisted. "You...it's like a cloud going over the sun, only in the earth, and you're drawing the earth-strength around you like you want to hide in it."

Thorazan held his tongue between his teeth to keep from saying more than he should. Of course Rhodri would be able to sense the feelings behind his words, just as Thorazan himself knew that the birdsong from those trees to the left, sweet and pleasant to the ear, was a furious cry of anger and challenge. At least earth-sense was only a matter of feeling, not Mind-speech: he was safe in saying, "None of your business."

Rhodri had less stamina than Thorazan had hoped. By noon the boy was flagging badly, and...Boys need to eat more often than grown men, and he has no reserves of flesh.

"I'm going to tie you to this tree and go hunting," Thorazan said. "Be assured that, if you try to escape, I shall find you and I shan't be as gentle as before."

"You can hit harder than that?" Rhodri said, green eyes wide. "But you're so small...Can you teach me how? Is it that a spell of strength is upon you?"

"It is the strength of my breeding," Thorazan replied. "No magic at all."

There is no law saying we must hate whom we war on, Thorazan thought, laying Rhodri down gently and unfastening his bedroll for the boy before he started the fire. He will be better off as playmate and servant to my son, well-fed and well-treated, than he was as the

Gwyrothi's heir. I captured him; after his information has been read from his mind, surely I may keep him. That thought had come to him quite early on - perhaps the first night...

"If you untied my legs, look you," Rhodri said as Thorazan began to gather wood for the fire, "I could help you with that, and the cooking as well."

"And not run?" Thorazan asked skeptically.

"You would catch me too quickly," the boy admitted. "Besides, my da says that a man does not do slaves' or women's work in his hall, but when men are out to war, even a chieftain must turn his hand to such tasks, lest his warriors think their honour lessened by serving him."

Thorazan considered a moment, but, truly, the boy had no chance of escaping. "I will have to tie you again before I sleep," he warned as he undid the knots. "But you may as well make yourself useful now."

Rhodri scampered about after dry branches while Thorazan chopped the wood with a small hatchet. The Plainsman peeled three juniper shoots to serve as primitive spits for the hare Thorazan had shot. Roast hare, its liver grilled separately and enough summer fat dripping from it to soak the hard little journey-cakes from Thorazan's pack; clean sweet water, and a moss-soft boulder big enough for both of them to lean against it while they cooked and ate...

Rhodri had found some wild garlic as well, pleasantly pungent on the meat; and outside the circle of light, fireflies darted flashing in the soft purple gloom. They ate in silence, the rustling sounds of the night-waking woodland stirring along their shared senses, and Thorazan felt peaceful as he had not for some time.

If only Thoramar were here! he thought. I wish my son could enjoy this as I do; but even without land-sense, it is a fair night. He and Rhodri should get on. Playmates now; and when Thoramar is old enough for military service, Rhodri will still be relatively young and active.

He is well-tempered enough: a little training, and...

"What are you going to do with me?" Rhodri asked, a sudden quiver of nervousness running through him like the ripples spreading from a fish's jump in a still pond.

"Take you to my home," Thorazan answered. "Get rid of all your lice and fleas..."

"Only sick people lose their lice and fleas," the boy protested.

Thorazan's scalp suddenly felt very itchy. "We do not keep bodily vermin," he said.

Although I likely have some of his now. "No lice, no fleas, no worms."

"Last month I made a bigger worm than anyone else in the clan's boy-troop," Rhodri boasted. Thorazan shuddered. A large dose, for both of us, as soon as we get back!

"You will be asked some questions - you need not fear!" he added as the boy suddenly tightened, eyes widening in terror. "We do not torture; only read the answers in your mind.

Then...if all goes well, I will take you home. You will have clean clothes every day, and a good bed, and your duties will be light, chiefly looking after my son Thoramar. You will like him, I think. He is close enough to your age, as we count it..."

"Is he as tall as I am?" Rhodri interrupted. "I am three inches over five feet already, and my da says I am like to grow another foot before I am done."

"Thoramar is near your height now, though I doubt he will be taller than I." Most Tharandrostans reached their full growth in early adolescence. "But he is heavier than you, and a good deal stronger."

"We'll see about that," Rhodri boasted. "I'll bet..." He paused, looking sideways - realized telling one's captor he can beat his son up is a bad idea, Thorazan thought, muffling his smile. The boy seemed extraordinarily bright for a Plainsman. But we have not bred our slaves for their intelligence. Wolves are brighter than lapdogs - and a wolf can be trained into a loyal hound, with time and care.

Rhodri slept quietly as Thorazan took the afternoon's game out of his backpack. He and

Rhodri had tickled trout together; the boy had taught him some of the useful plants up here with which Thorazan was unfamiliar; and... there had been fairly long stretches of time in which one or both of them had forgotten that they were captor and captive.

Once they had needed to hide from a small band of outlaws, but the woods concealed them. The robbers had passed right by where they stood, arguing over the footprints. Rhodri's oversized feet, bearing little weight, were clearly a boy's; the outlaws had mistaken the Tharandrostan's shorter, slimmer prints for a woman's.

What they had bragged of their plans for both had tempted Thorazan to risk taking them all on in hopes of cleaning the world a little. For his mission's sake, he had restrained himself; but the experience convinced Rhodri that his captor was also his protector. Thorazan could leave the boy untied at night, even give him a knife to clean fish and game with. Save for the added delight of sharing earth-sense with Rhodri, Thorazan thought, much of their journey truly had been like going hunting with his own son.

Until early that evening, when Commander Darzarak had spoken into Thorazan's mind again, demanding a report. Thorazan had given it to him as briefly and clearly as he could, and received his commander's sober approval. Well-done. Your captive is the only one of the Gwyrothi's heirs with land-sense. And apparently that is a requirement for the chieftain; otherwise the clan is ruled by a council of 'royal' relatives and Oak-Men; and that is a receipt for chaos.

Removing this whelp will prove a great aid. But hasten as swiftly as you may! After ther last defeat, the Gwyrothi scattered into small bands hiding in the woods and mountains. They would die to keep your captive out of our hands, if they could. They know that they can bargain for prisoners with Kantar, whereas we have a longer view of the situation.

The short discussion had left Thorazan with a feeling of unease that would not come clear in his mind, though he was unsure why. He chopped the meat into cubes, stringing it on skewers with the savoury herbs he had collected as they walked, and began to roast it over the fire, trying to dig the reason for his disturbance out of his mind.

As the scent of cooking meat wafted across to him, Rhodri sat up, knuckling sleep from his green eyes. Something prickled at the back of Thorazan's thoughts...Our tame Plainsmen are mostly blue-eyed. Or brown or hazel; but I have never seen a green-eyed one before, except that one Oak-Man...

"Your eyes," the Tharandrostan said musingly, almost as if talking to himself. Rhodri looked curiously at him. "Do many of your tribe have green eyes?"

17

"Only us with earth-sense or the Sight," Rhodri answered at once. "And most of us who have magic are green-eyed, too. It's how the Oak-Men knew I was special since I was a wean."

Thorazan sucked in a deep gasp of air, as though he had taken a hard blow to the belly.

That one blow jarred everything into place in his mind: he felt as though, having stared at a painting so closely as to see only splotches of colour and brush-swirls, he had suddenly taken a step back so that the whole image could solidify before his eyes. He had gotten a good briefing before coming up here, every soldier had - including the warning about green eyes as a marker trait for mind-gifts and magic.

I will never be able to take him home, Thorazan realized. All I told him, all the promises of kind treatment and good food and warm clothes - it was all lies. And, if he sees the blow coming, he will die knowing I betrayed him.

"What's wrong?" Rhodri asked. "Is it outlaws again?" The soles of Thorazan's feet prickled, picking up the young Plainsman's sudden terror vibrating through the ground.

"No. Quite...not."

"But..."

"There is no danger right now. Eat your dinner quietly, please. I need to think." I need not to think. If I had a barrel of wine...I cannot bear this. I must bring him back, but...

If he escaped now...By rights, if Thorazan let his captive go, he would have earned a traitor's punishment. Kantar executed its betrayers by hanging, drawing and quartering; Tharandrost was more subtle.

Absently Thorazan touched his head. The State would not waste the fertile seed of a pureblood who had successfully fathered a child; they would not kill his body. Instead, Mind-Healers would examine his thoughts closely, seeking out the flaws that had led to his actions.

They would remove those flaws - burn out his earth-sense, if it seemed a real factor.

Certainly he would no longer be allowed to scout by himself, even if he kept his talent.

And they would probably take the memory of what he had done. Or else change his mind so that he would remember only shame: the appalling degradation of living in his own filth in the woods like a louse-ridden Plainsman, so lost to sanity as to think a worm-riddled wile whelp would make a fit companion for his own son.

But it was more likely that Thorazan would simply live knowing that he had shamed himself and his nation, but never knowing how. And...all he had ever been trained for was scouting. If Thorazan lost his Mind-gift, he would be good only for the simplest record-keeping, or retraining as a front-line soldier. At best, his pay would be halved; if he were thrown out, the best job a disgraced man could hope for would be as deckhand on a small fishing boat.

His family's minds would be scrutinized as well...Thorazan could see Thoramar's bright amber-gray eyes dulling with disappointment and shame, his son who had always been so proud of his father; he could see the tears shining on Indamith's delicate cheeks. Thoramar had hoped to be a squire someday, perhaps even in the Silent Guard. There would be no chance for that, if Thorazan disgraced himself so badly: no knight would take a boy from a shamed family.

You, or my son, Thorazan thought, looking across the fire at Rhodri. The world was full of Plainsmen...too full, considering what they had done at Flintwall Keep and a number of places like it. How could he free a boy who might grow up to lead another host of rapists and woman-murderers in another generation?

How can I deliver Rhodri's trust to death?

How can I let his life destroy my family's?

For a moment, Thorazan thought that perhaps he should disappear, take Rhodri and head back into the woods and never come out. But his country would find him, no matter how far he ran: the land could hide his body, but not his mind. The stars shone bright above the little clearing, cool and far away. I will find no help there, Thorazan thought. The gods did not move Men, only offered choices. And if he prayed to Aviyani for aid... she was the giver of earth-sense, Lady of all that lived, and source of the might of the land. The wolf might slay the deer, the fox the rabbit, without fear of godly retribution. But lies and betrayal were another thing - and Rhodri believed all Thorazan had told him.

"Look you, are you sure I can't help?" Rhodri said softly. "You look so...so..."

Only twelve years old, Thorazan thought. A toddler's age; but he is a child verging on manhood. By the time Thoramar's life is a third done, Rhodri would be eighty-seven, and likely dying of old age; in the wild, he could hardly live that long. He is more likely to be dead before fifty, even if he survives this war. A stupid, stupid gamble: three long lives ruined, for one short one saved...perhaps no more than a month or two.

"Did you not say we would be with your people soon?" Rhodri said curiously. "No need for you to be so downcast, now. It's been a grand journey, most of it. My da hasn't the earthsight, and the Oak-Men hadn't often time to spend with me when they could be training apprentices." The boy's high wistful voice was almost a whisper, as though he hoped no one could overhear his admission.

Thorazan's dam broke. He pressed his hands tight against the thin steel cap under his hood, rocking back and forth. I can't, he cried silently to himself. I can't!

Rhodri got up, came over to put a skinny arm around his shoulders. "What's wrong?" he asked again.

Thorazan swallowed hard, looked straight into the boy's leaf-green eyes. Dirty as Rhodri's face was, Thorazan could already see the lines of a man's features emerging: his strong chin and jaw, his proud cheekbones, his broad brow. He could be...Great among his own folk; a danger to mine. And yet...

"Rhodri," he said, the first time he had called the young Plainsman by name, "I lied."

Rhodri flinched. "About what?"

"I lied to myself," Thorazan admitted, the words bursting from him like festering poison from a wound. "I was told what your colouring meant...but I hid it from my mind because, because I was already coming to think..." Coming to think of you as a child instead of an animal, in truth. "Rhodri, I never saw a green-eyed Plainsman in Tharandrost because we cull all our slaves with any hint of magic or Mind-gift. If I bring you back, you will be killed as well. And if I don't...I will suffer a traitor's fate." The State might even take Thoramar away from him, and let him see his wife only at the House of Procreation every three to five years, whenever she ripened an egg. If at all; if they didn't decide that the taint was in his blood rather than his mind...And separation might actually be best, to preserve Thoramar and Indamith from his shame.

Rhodri stared in shock, but his grip tightened around Thorazan's broad shoulders. "So...your son, your house..."

"It was all true, except the hope that you might come with me. That was the lie I told myself, and believing it, you as well."

"And if you don't bring me to die, then you must die yourself?"

"Not die, probably, but..." Words tumbling out of his mouth like rocks racing downhill into an avalanche, Thorazan told Rhodri what would happen to himself. By the end, tears were running down the boy's face.

"You shouldn't of told me that," Rhodri whispered, clinging to him. "If you'd just brought me...Don't take me to them, at least. If I've got to die, let your hand send me to Gwyddyd's Wood, so I can get there safe and come back to the green earth with a clean soul."

Thorazan found that he, too, was weeping without shame. No grown man - no belted knight of the highest Imperial blood - could meet his fate more bravely than this Plainsman child. And that, in turn, made Thorazan certain of what he must do. He swallowed hard, blew his nose on his cloak.

"No," he said. "I am setting you free - in return for an oath. Someday you will lead your people; you have it in you, I think, to be a great leader. But I have seen what wild Plainsmen do in war." As evenly as he could manage, Thorazan told Rhodri what he had seen at Flintwall Keep, and heard of elsewhere. "Swear to me, by Aviyani and Gwyddyd, by your love of the green earth and the life I am returning to you, that you will never allow such things to be done so long as your strength and life can stand in the way. I cannot ask you to swear never to make war, for Amanvon alone knows what lies before us. But if you must - make sure that it is war, not savagery, not butchery of the innocent, not destruction of women and children. Will you swear?"

"I will," said Rhodri firmly. "By Aviyani and Gwyddyd, by my love of the green earth and the life you give me." To Thorazan's surprise, the boy kissed him firmly on the mouth - a Plainsman's salute to a beloved chieftain, or a father. Thorazan emptied his pack, looking at its contents. The boy could not carry much: journeycakes, Thorazan's knife, his camp hatchet, and his case of medicine would have to do.

He explained each of the medications, finishing with, "These three dried berries are darvarberries. Don't take more than - hmm, a quarter of one - at the same time every day. That will keep you awake and strong. But you must be in a safe place when they run out, because you will sleep for as long as you were wakeful. Now, go to your people. And be very careful," he added grimly as the last, worst possibility came to his mind. "For, to expiate what I have done- it is possible that my superiors could set mind-bonds of compulsion on me and send me out again to hunt you down."

"I understand," Rhodri murmured. "I will be careful. And...You never told me your name."

"Thorazan Thoramarun."

"Thorazan Thoramarun." The boy pronounced the foreign sounds gingerly, as though fearing they would break in his mouth. "Even if your people make you forget - I'll remember for you. There will be songs of this...and those we spare, if I am Gwyrothi in wartime, will know it is for your sake."

"Go now, Rhodri, and the gods be with you. Run!"

Rhodri ran, leaping and twisting through the darkness like a deer. Thorazan felt the boy long after he was out of sight, flowing through the shifting patterns of trees and roots, streams and rocks without a single misstep. But finally Rhodri reached the furthest edge of the Tharandrostan's awareness, and was gone.

Thorazan tied up his bedroll and doused the fire. He sat in the darkness, letting his thoughts melt into the earth around him, until birdsong prickled along the edge of his hearing and light began to seep through the canopy of leaves above him. He drew his sword, watching the dawn's brightness break off its well-honed edge. It would be better for me, if...

The point touched his chest, rested there a moment. Then he shook his head. It might well take the two hundred years or so that remained of his life for him to repay his country for what he had done: he had made his choice, and would not flee his atonement. Thorazan rose, stiff, sore, and damp from sitting so long, and began to walk, back to whatever judgement his deed might bring upon him.

"Once to every man and nation,
Comes the power to decide,
In the strife of True and Twisted,
For the good or evil side..."

- "Once to Every Man and Nation", in Prince Avalar's Hymns,
ed. Noril Marsathar, #23

TALE CONTINUED IN EMPIRE'S GHOST

BIOGRAPHY

K.Gundarsson: June 28, 1967 - Sept 29, 2021

From his humble beginnings, Gundarsson would make his mark on the world by writing on the most rare and obscure myths breathing new life into them, for a new generation of readers. His fictional works written under Stephan Grundy focused on mythology and history and were met with international success. Along with his fictional works, Gundarsson made a name for himself writing books on Germanic Paganism (also known as heathenry) and Germanic Culture.

He is an Elder in the organization The Troth where he has dedicated a majority of his life influencing major changes in the organization, including the development of anti-racist and anti-sexist ideals. He has fought for equality in trans-gendered communities, as well as fighting for the acceptance of Loki. Gundarsson has shaped heathenry through his numerous academic and fictional works as well as his extensive articles, thesis papers and his creation and sustainment of the lore program within The Troth. His hobbies included wood-working, jewelry making and gardening as well as historical re-enactment.

The Three Little Sisters

The Three Little Sisters is an indie publisher that puts authors first. We specalize in the strange and unusual. From titles about pagan and heathen spirituality to traditional fiction we bring books to life.

https://the3littlesisters.com